CLEOPATRA QUEEN OF PEBBLE BEACH

A True Story

Enjoy!
Suzanne Lehr

Have fun!
Mary Wurtz

❧ FIRST EDITION ❧

By **Suzanne Lehr** & **Mary Wurtz**
Illustrated by **Joel Anderson**

Publishers Cataloging-in-Publication Data

Lehr, Suzanne.
    Cleopatra, queen of Pebble Beach : a true story / by Suzanne Lehr & Mary
Wurtz ; illustrated by Joel Anderson.
        p. cm.
    Summary: Describes the real-life antics of a basset hound named Cleopatra
and how she charmed the community of Pebble Beach, California, during the
1980s.
    ISBN-13: 978-1-60131-072-9
    [1. Basset hound. 2. Basset hound —Biography. 3. Dogs —Anecdotes.
4. Dogs —Anecdotes —Juvenile literature. 5. Pebble Beach (Calif.) —Social life
and customs.] I. Wurtz, Mary. II. Anderson, Joel, ill. III. Title.
                                                              2010933060

Copyright © 2010 Suzanne Lehr and Mary Wurtz
Printed and bound in the United States of America
First printing 2010
For additional information please go to www.SPCAmc.org

115 Bluebill Drive
Savannah, GA 31419
United States
(888) 300-1961

This book was published with the assistance of the helpful folks at DragonPencil.com.

❧ PREFACE ☙

This is a true story. It happened in Pebble Beach, California. The children featured and the places mentioned are real. While children of all ages will enjoy this book, parents and grandparents will take great pleasure in reading it to young children.

The idea for this book came about at a dinner party, where the hosts began telling "dog stories" about their basset hound. The stories relayed were utterly charming. The next day one of the guests proposed making this story come to life by creating a book where 100% of the proceeds would go to the local SPCA—Society for the Prevention of Cruelty to Animals. Cleopatra, the star of this book, found her way to the Monterey SPCA, where she waited to be discovered by a loving family.

The SPCA for Monterey County was started in 1905 to address the problem of stray "dogs and cats around town". It is a nonprofit, independent, donor-supported humane society that shelters homeless, neglected, and abused pets and animals of many kinds.

❧ ACKNOWLEDGMENTS ☙

Thanks to the Lehr family, whose children shared many wonderful memories of their adventures with Cleo. A special thanks to Elisa, who framed the story and repeatedly helped to make an enchanting tale. Many friends read various drafts and added their comments, improving the storyline. To Madge Palumbo, Virginia Stone, M.C. and Leni Eccles, Carol Mollman, Dr. Louise Stanger, our editor Susan Shami, and our illustrator Joel Anderson, we send our heartfelt thanks.

We hope you enjoy reading this tale as much as we enjoyed writing it.

Three days before Christmas, in a certain house on Alva Lane in Pebble Beach, California, preparations were well under way. However, the children were still stumped—what could they possibly get their doctor dad? He worked long hours, played tennis, jogged, and loved animals, especially their golden retriever, Winston. Dr. Dad really didn't need anything.

While watching TV one day, the older children—Elisa, age ten, and Alexandra, age seven—spotted an advertisement from the SPCA: "... *homeless puppies desperately in need of good homes*." Immediately the children bubbled with excitement. "A puppy!" Elisa shrieked. "That's it. It's the perfect gift for Dad!" The younger siblings, Vanessa and Ryan, also loved the idea. They proceeded to convince Mom that they must go to the SPCA right away. Mother shepherded Elisa, Alexandra, Vanessa, Ryan, and Winston into the old Jeep, and off they went.

Upon arriving, the children peered into the rows of caged dogs—young, old, yipping, jumping, lying quietly, looking sad, and all deserving of a good home. Vanessa, who was five years old and had a devilish personality, long blond hair, huge eyes, and a loud voice that could convince anyone of anything, skipped ahead. Suddenly, she stopped and shouted, "I've found it! I love this puppy!"

Ryan, age three, rushed to her side and immediately joined in, yelling, "I want this dog, Mama. I love it!"

Everyone hurried to the last cage. In it was the saddest-looking dog they had ever seen. As she lumbered toward the children, her pendulous ears were swinging, grazing the floor. Drool hung from her mouth, and the whites of her sad eyes shone beneath her big brown pupils.

This puppy had been found in front of the building, covered with filth and grease, without a collar or identification. She had been given a bath and was patiently waiting for someone to take her home.

Mom filled out the appropriate forms and received instructions from the attendant. Off they went with their newly found gift. Everyone was excited, including Winston, who at long last had a playmate. "Dad is going to LOVE this present!" exclaimed Vanessa.

Christmas morning, Dad was completely shocked, but totally charmed by his gift. On the dog's collar was a message saying, "I love treats of all kinds!" Dad immediately went to "the cookie pouch," he gave the dog a treat, and the attachment was instant!

The next challenge was naming this pup. She managed to convey, with her slow, purposeful gait and tail held high in the air, both an attitude of superiority and a sense of noblesse oblige. Her demeanor suggested that she was "to the manor born." She had the bearing of a queen. Everyone had heard of Cleopatra, Queen of the Nile, who, like most monarchs of her era, saw herself as divine from birth. Cleopatra, Queen of Pebble Beach, was the perfect name! All who came to know her fondly called her Cleo.

Vanessa proudly took Cleo, after barely a month with the family, to the Blessing of the Animals at All Saints' Day School. In a touching ceremony, children brought their animals to the schoolyard to be blessed. Dogs, cats, goats, rabbits, fish, rats, birds, and, yes, even butterflies were marched or carried around the playground by their proud owners. Each pet received a blessing. Cleo would not cooperate and had no intention of waiting for a blessing. Breaking loose from Vanessa's grip, she ran directly into the Early Childhood Unit, where snacks were laid out. She got her squat legs up on a low bench and proceeded to clear the unsupervised table of goldfish crackers, cookies, and all other things edible. It became apparent that Cleo was nature's best vacuum cleaner. While she appreciated her new family, her first priority was definitely her stomach.

Cleopatra was not a barker, but could she howl! Actually, this family found howling less annoying than barking. When Vanessa practiced her violin or the older girls played the piano, Cleo would howl and, depending on the song, she was more or less on key. Through trial and error, "Home On the Range" became her favorite. Cleo could show off the full range of her "operatic" style, as the highs and lows were rewarded with liver treats.

Although Cleo loved the family, her wandering spirit could not be fenced. The children took her for daily walks, and Dad attempted to have her accompany him on his neighborhood jogs. But, unlike Winston, Cleo was not a jogger and preferred to travel solo. Friends were aware of Cleo's tendency to wander, and "Cleo sightings" were frequent.

One morning, the family was awakened by Vanessa's shrieks. "Yikes! We have two Cleos!" It did not take long to figure out that the basset with the white around the tail was Alexander, another local pet. But how had he gotten into the house? While driving home after having dinner in The Tap Room, some friends had almost run over a basset hound that they assumed was Cleo. Because it was late, they just let her in through the sliding door. Everyone had a good laugh before returning Alexander to his rightful residence.

As Cleopatra became increasingly comfortable in her new environment, she began to explore, highly motivated by her insatiable dual appetites for food and adventure. The air was full of enticing food smells wafting from the various kitchens in The Lodge. The grounds became a natural place for her to wander. Her preferred route was out the back gate, but when it was closed, she would sneak through the front gate, somehow spreading her toes to maneuver over the five-foot cattle guard. Her wanderings became known as "Cleo's Grand Rounds."

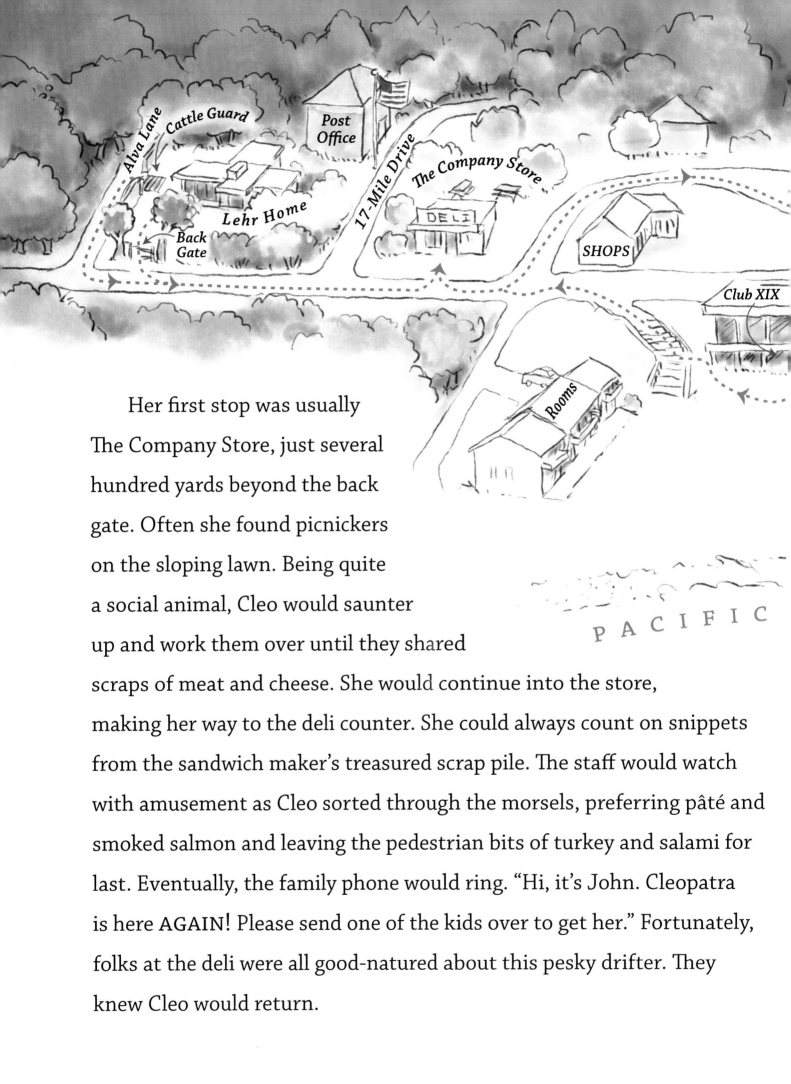

Her first stop was usually
The Company Store, just several
hundred yards beyond the back
gate. Often she found picnickers
on the sloping lawn. Being quite
a social animal, Cleo would saunter
up and work them over until they shared
scraps of meat and cheese. She would continue into the store,
making her way to the deli counter. She could always count on snippets
from the sandwich maker's treasured scrap pile. The staff would watch
with amusement as Cleo sorted through the morsels, preferring pâté and
smoked salmon and leaving the pedestrian bits of turkey and salami for
last. Eventually, the family phone would ring. "Hi, it's John. Cleopatra
is here AGAIN! Please send one of the kids over to get her." Fortunately,
folks at the deli were all good-natured about this pesky drifter. They
knew Cleo would return.

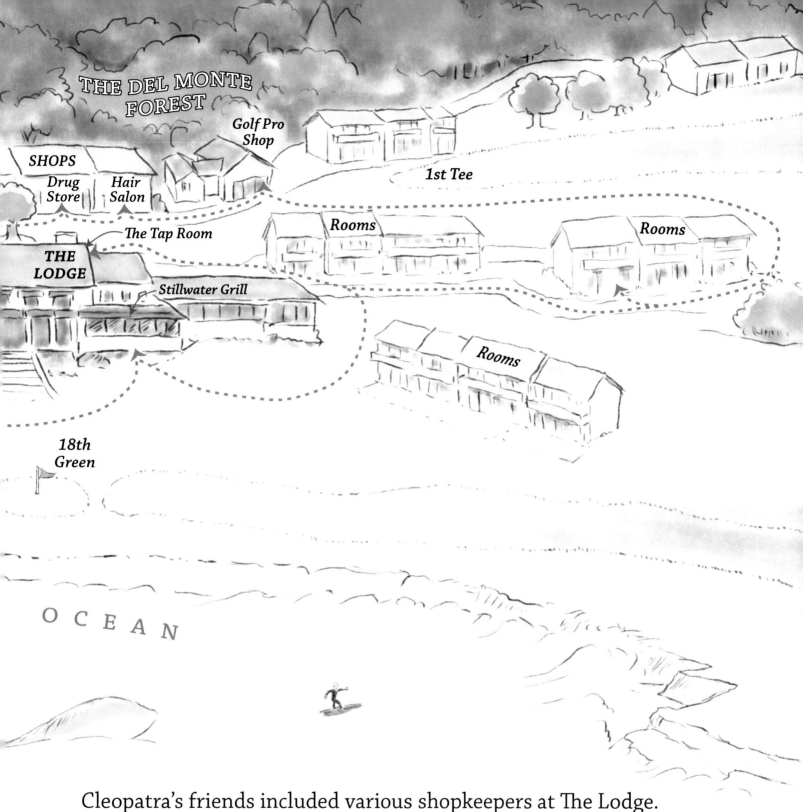

Cleopatra's friends included various shopkeepers at The Lodge. After The Company Store, her travels would take her to The Drug Store. At the soda fountain counter, she would look longingly at whoever was sitting on the high stool and howl "Home on the Range," always a bit off key. Tourists fell for the act hook, line, and sinker. Cleo was rewarded with bits of ice cream cones, sandwiches, and other sweet treats.

After a quick stop at the hair salon, where she had trained the staff to bring her treats, she would mosey over to The Golf Pro Shop, greeting golfers and charming new acquaintances. Cleopatra knew from experience that these tourists might invite her to their hotel room, where a new adventure and often a feast would await. Room service was her favorite. Periodically, she would meander along the hallways looking for discarded trays. She would nudge the silver covers off the plates, revealing sumptuous leftovers.

As an expert wanderer, Cleo knew that she must keep moving. Cleopatra, the slow but determined "Queen of Pebble Beach," became a stealthy, deliberate, and mysterious female. Countless times the children would hightail it to The Company Store only to be told, "She was just here a moment ago. She can't be far."

Cleo learned the routines of the various restaurants at The Lodge and The Beach Club. She knew that Sunday afternoon was the best time to hit Stillwater Grill to partake of leftovers from the succulent Sunday brunch. She had a taste for seafood, loved quiche, and never met a pastry she didn't like. The staff knew and loved Cleo. In fact, the children were convinced that some of the staff conspired to help her keep her whereabouts a secret. "Sorry, kids, haven't seen Cleo today," the doorman at The Lodge would say with a twinkle in his eye. It was easier to turn a blind eye to her meanderings, not bothering to dial the numbers prominently displayed on her tag. But all the switchboard operators knew Cleo's phone number by heart.

Late night hunger pangs would draw Cleo slowly but deftly down the driveway and over the cattle guard, under the cloak of darkness, to reach the garbage cans behind Club XIX. The French chef and his sous chef did not find Cleopatra the least bit charming and would angrily shoo her from the kitchen. Occasionally a message was found on the family answering machine and played over and over. "The BEAST! She is here again! Kindly remove her from the premises and control your animal."

The Tap Room, a casual and dog-friendly place, was another haunt. The waitstaff kept her occupied with day-old desserts. Occasionally a photo would show up of Cleo sharing a cheeseburger and fries with a foursome of raucous golfers.

One night Cleo did not return home, which was unusual. After three days, everyone in the family, including Winston, began to worry. Friends were called and the children began to make and distribute flyers throughout Pebble Beach. The family desperately contacted all of Cleo's favorite haunts: The Company Store, The Golf Pro Shop, the hair salon, The Drug Store, and The Tap Room. "No, she hasn't been here for several days," was the recurring response. Even the Chef at Club XIX was missing the mournful beggar. In fact, the entire Pebble Beach community joined in the search.

Sunday night arrived, and there was still no sign of the infamous queen-like canine. Suddenly, the phone rang, interrupting a rather somber dinner. As Dad answered it, the family listened intently to the one-sided conversation. They watched Dad's eyes get bigger and bigger. At one point, he looked quite alarmed and began stammering an apology. Then he began to roar with laughter, tears rolling down his cheeks. The children exchanged puzzled looks. Dad hung up the phone and, still laughing, proceeded to describe a most unbelievable scene.

Cleopatra had snuck into one of the wedding reception rooms in The Lodge at Pebble Beach, which was all set up and waiting for the guests and newlyweds to enter. There, before her eyes, was the most delicious-looking thing she had ever seen: an intricate seven-layer wedding cake, beautifully decorated . . . and definitely within reach! That fearless thief climbed up on the low table and began to dig in. The kitchen staff discovered her gobbling up the cake, when the top layers collapsed on her, covering her in buttercream and flowers. "OH NO, YOU NASTY DOG!" the wedding planner screamed as she dashed off to alert the newlyweds. Luckily, the bride and groom were serious animal lovers with a great sense of humor. (French pastries were served in lieu of cake.)

Extremely embarrassed, the family arrived to apologize to the newlyweds and to collect their incorrigible dog. As the children ran and hugged the "frosted beast," the couple explained their previous meetings with Cleo. It turned out that Cleo had been a guest in their honeymoon suite all weekend, dining on room service meals and sleeping by the fire. They had fallen in love with Cleo and wanted to bring her home to start their new life together. The family stood firm. Cleopatra was not for sale! Besides, as Dad explained, Cleopatra belonged not only to their family; she was an iconic mascot of Pebble Beach.

To own a basset hound such as Cleopatra, one has to have a great deal of humility, patience, and an even greater sense of humor. Cleo was hard to see, creeping through the dark streets, and cars hit her several times. In spite of her travails, she lived to be fourteen (ninety-eight in human years) as the unofficial mascot and the Queen of the Pebble Beach community. The enchanted forest-by-the-sea, Pebble Beach, was Cleopatra's "kingdom," and stories of her "reign" exist to this day. Her family and the residents, employees, and resort guests during the 1980s have fond memories of Cleopatra, the regal, meandering basset hound.

❧ ABOUT THE AUTHORS ❧

SUZANNE LEHR was born and raised in New York City. A practicing psychologist, she and her husband moved to Pebble Beach 37 years ago and never looked back. Her greatest achievements are her four children and four grandchildren. Suzanne is an active community leader and currently lives in Carmel with her husband and 14-year-old golden retriever.

MARY WURTZ lives in Carmel, California, with her husband Don and their Pembroke Welsh corgi. She is a mother, grandmother of three, fine art photographer, former teacher, and president of the Carmel Public Library Foundation. She is currently devoting her energy toward bringing the El Sistema USA program to Salinas, California.